Keep On Wheeling

By Samantha Wasserman

To order additional copies of this book, contact:
Xlibris
844-714-8691
www.Xlibris.com
Orders@Xlibris.com

ISBN: Softcover   979-8-3694-1264-0
        Hardcover   979-8-3694-1265-7
        EBook   979-8-3694-1263-3

Library of Congress Control Number: 2023923115

Print information available on the last page

Rev. date: 01/23/2024

Dedication

For my mom. I am only here because of your support and love. There aren't enough thank yous.

Daddy, grandma, and the real Oscar,
this is my test of courage.

Reese was told she needed a wheelchair.

Her brother, Oscar, tried to imagine
still doing fun things together.

"Help, I'm sinking!"
yelled Reese.

"What if no one plays with me at recess?" Reese fretted.

Oscar didn't understand Reese's wheelchair.

So they put their thinking caps
on and did research.

"Reese, we have so many things
to try!" Oscar yelled excitedly.

Reese learned about wheelchair sports.

"Hockey! Basketball! Too many to choose."

And found tips for the
best backyard camping.

Reese compiled riddles to prove she'll always be funnier than Oscar.

What does the plate say to the fork?

Dinner's on me.

Why do dogs lick us?

They smell bones inside.

What's a deer with no eyes?

No eye-deer.

How does the butcher introduce his wife?

Meat Patty.

Oscar researched the 1990s so they could "travel" back in time.

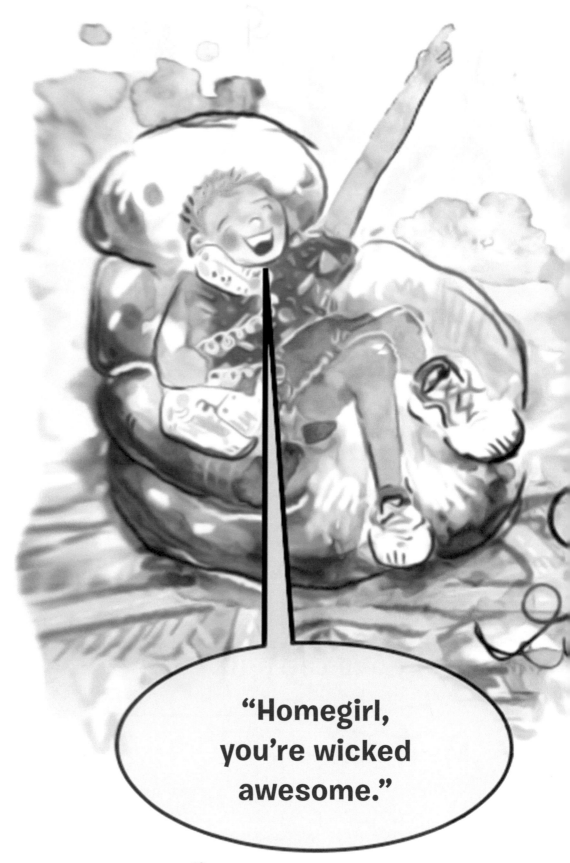

"Homegirl, you're wicked awesome."

"I'll always *stand* up for what's right."

“And nothing will keep me from flying.”

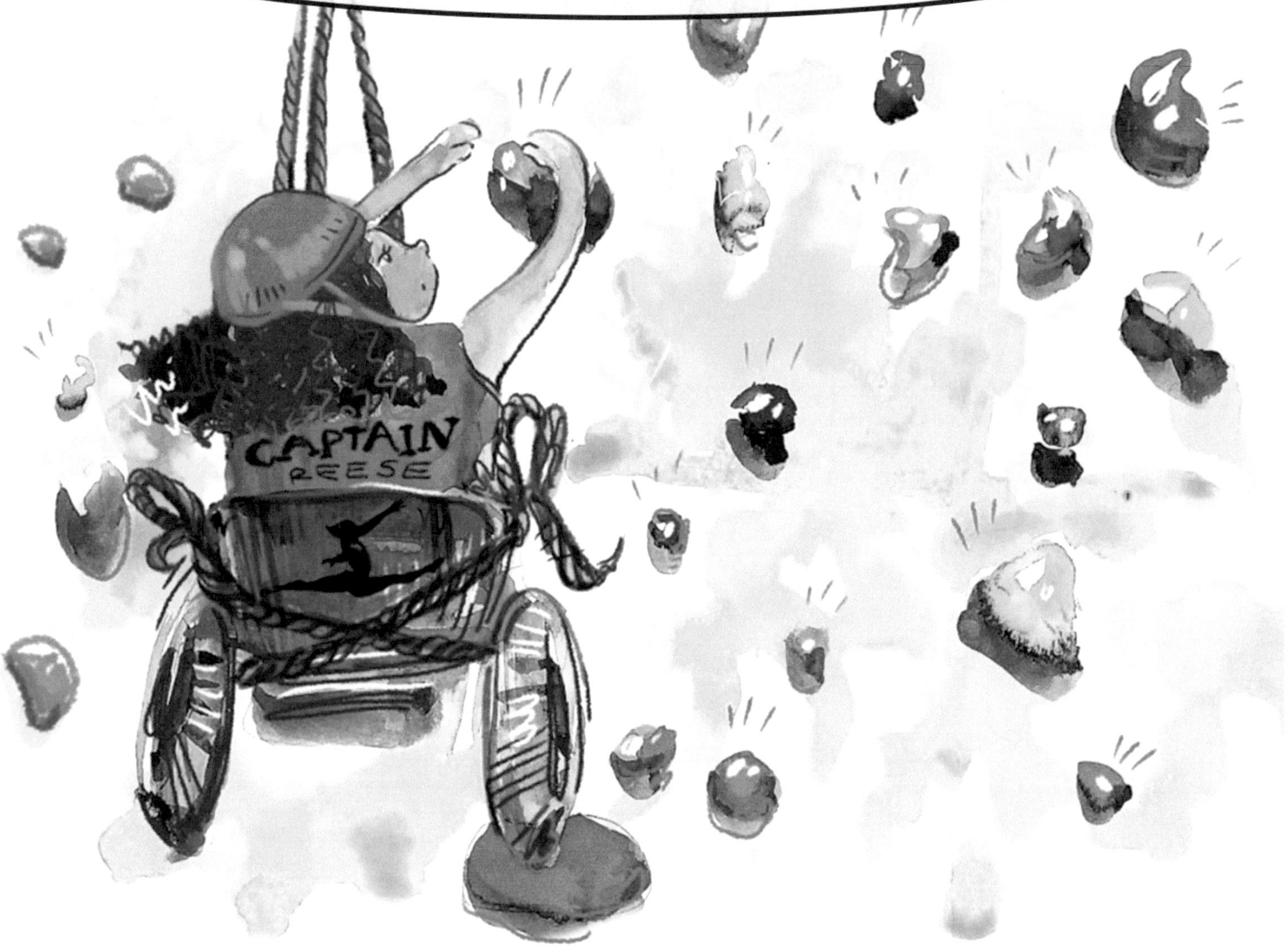

Reese and Oscar are the strongest team now, and forever.

What should their first adventure be?

 KeepWheeling1

Samantha lives in Washington, DC, where she worked for the Federal Government across four Departments – Defense, Homeland Security, Transportation, and Health and Human Services – for over a decade. She currently spends her time writing and working on her recovery.

note from the author

I was diagnosed with multiple sclerosis in 2007, at age 22. I started using a cane in 2014, but within a year, I needed more support, I needed a wheelchair. I literally couldn't get places, and the more I thought a cane was enough, the more I missed. I lost friends and my connection to the community, as well as my job. By 2017, I couldn't do it anymore, that is when I knew I needed to suck it up and get a wheelchair. I refused it for so many years, but when I got it, I instantly felt free. The wheelchair saved me. Ironically, the wheelchair sent me off to the races. But yes, there are friends who still leave me out.

Kids, be patient with your friends in wheelchairs. Find ways to include them where everybody has fun. And if you're in a wheelchair, get creative with ways you can participate. It is not easy, but just remember how strong you are, and how much you can accomplish.

Thank you to my doctors who helped get me here:
Todd Cox, Peter Calabrasi, Nancy Hu, Moira Baynes, Heidi Crayton, Laxman Bahroo, Robert Mordkin, Christopher McMackin, Kunwardeep Sohal, Bruce Bonn, Michael Benjamin Lee.